THE BABY BEEBEE BIRD

Diane Redfield Massie · PICTURES BY Steven Kellogg

NEW TO THE ZOO

For Daniel and Leanna Hardy
—D.R.M.

To Peter with love
—S.K.

The Baby Beebee Bird   Text copyright © 1963 by Diane Redfield Massie   Illustrations copyright © 2000 by Steven Kellogg   Manufactured in China.   All rights reserved.   www.harperchildrens.com Library of Congress Cataloging-in-Publication Data   Massie, Diane Redfield.   The baby beebee bird / by Diane Redfield Massie ; pictures by Steven Kellogg.   p.   cm.   Summary: The zoo animals find a way to keep the baby beebee bird awake during the day so that they can get some sleep at night. ISBN 0-06-028083-2. — ISBN 0-06-028084-0 (lib. bdg.) — ISBN 0-06-051784-0 (pbk.)   [1. Zoo animals—Fiction.   2. Sleep—Fiction.]   I. Kellogg, Steven, ill.   II. Title.   PZ7.M42385Bag 2000 99-33421   [E]—dc21   CIP   AC   Typography by Michele N. Tupper

Newly Illustrated Edition

HarperCollins*Publishers*

R

EEEEEEEEEEEK EEK EEEEK

AKKKITY AK

AK

AK

EEEEK

a

arga

a

hissssssssss

The animals at the zoo had roared
and growled and hissed and meowed
all day long. They were very tired.

abba babba

abba babba

ba

bba

hissssssss hisssssssss hisssss

hissssssss

"It's eight o'clock," yawned the elephant,
and he settled down in his big hay bed.
"I've eaten 562 peanuts today," he said.

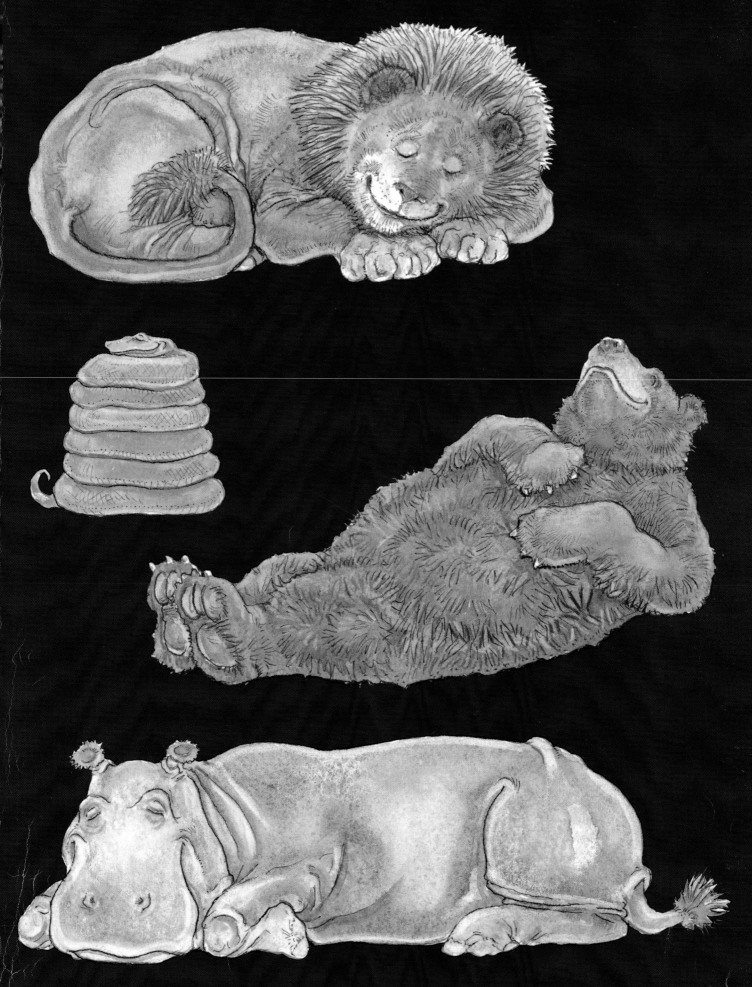

But no one heard him. They were all asleep.

The zoo was very still . . . until . . .

"What,"

said the elephant,

"is THAT?"

"It's the baby beebee
bird," said the giraffe.
"He's new to the zoo."

"Well, tell him to be QUIET,"
growled the leopard.
"I want to sleep."

beebeebobbibobbi beebeebobbibobbi

"Be quiet, please," said the giraffe politely.

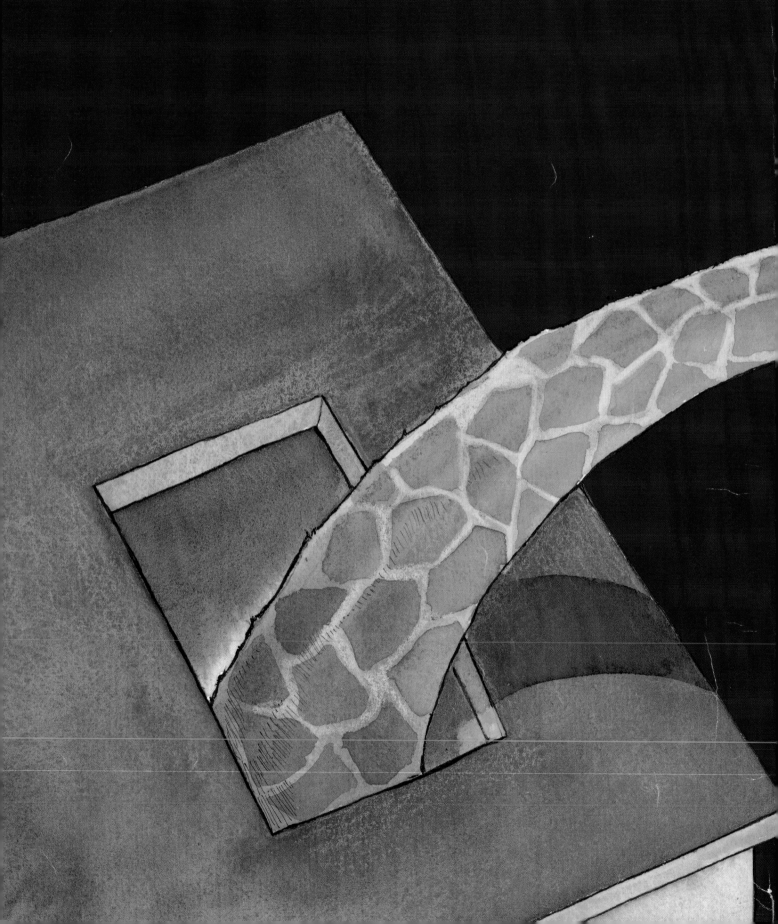

beebeebobbibobbi beebeebobbibobbi

"QUIET!"

roared the lion.

"He's wide awake,"
explained the giraffe.

"Why isn't he tired
like the rest of us?"
moaned the bear.

beebeebobbibobbi beebeebobbibobbi

"Aren't you tired?" asked the giraffe.

"No," said the beebee bird. "I've slept all day, and now it's time for me to SING. . . ."

beebeebobbibobbi beebeebobbibobbi

"Oh dear," said the elephant, "and I am so sleepy."

beebeebobbibobbi beebeebobbibobbi

"QUIET!" shouted all the animals.

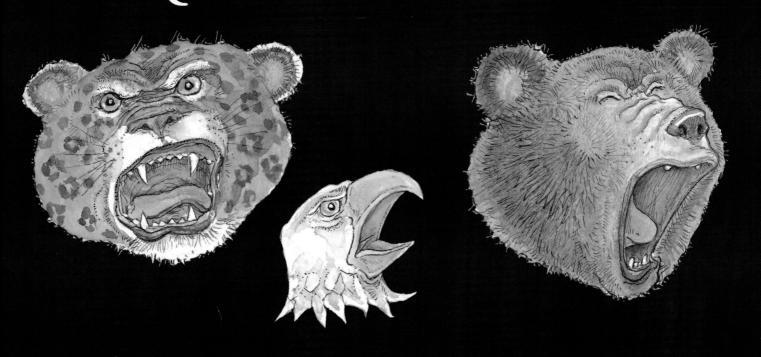

beebeebobbibobbi beebeebobbibobbi

beebeebobbibobbi beebeebobbibobbi

"WE CAN'T SLEEP!!!"

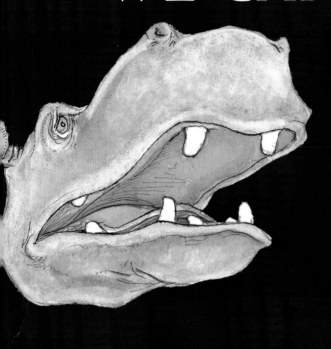
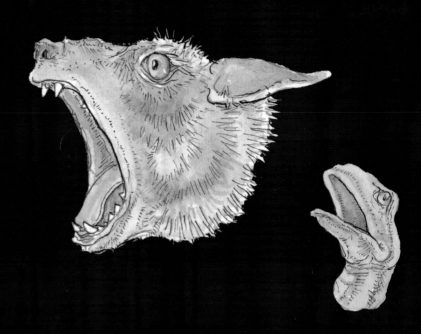

beebeebobbibobbi beebeebobbibobbi

all

night

long.

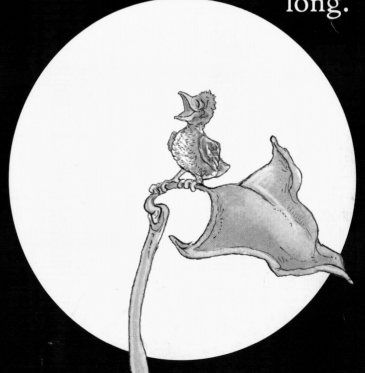

The sun rose in the morning on a very tired zoo.
"What can be the matter?" cried the keeper.
"The elephant is still lying down."

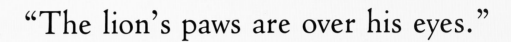
"The lion's paws are over his eyes."

"The eagle
isn't
screeching."

"Oh, dear me, the animals must be sick!" he wailed.

And he hurried away.

"Beebeebobbibobbi," said the baby beebee bird cheerfully, and he settled down for his morning nap.

beebee
bobbibobbi
beebeezz zzzzzzzzzzzzzzzzzz

The lion
whispered
to the bear.
"I have a plan,"
he said.

The bear
nodded,
and
whispered
the plan
to the others.

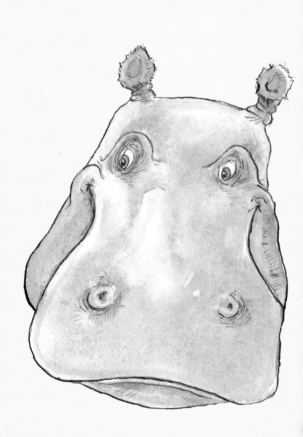

The beebee bird
was at last asleep.

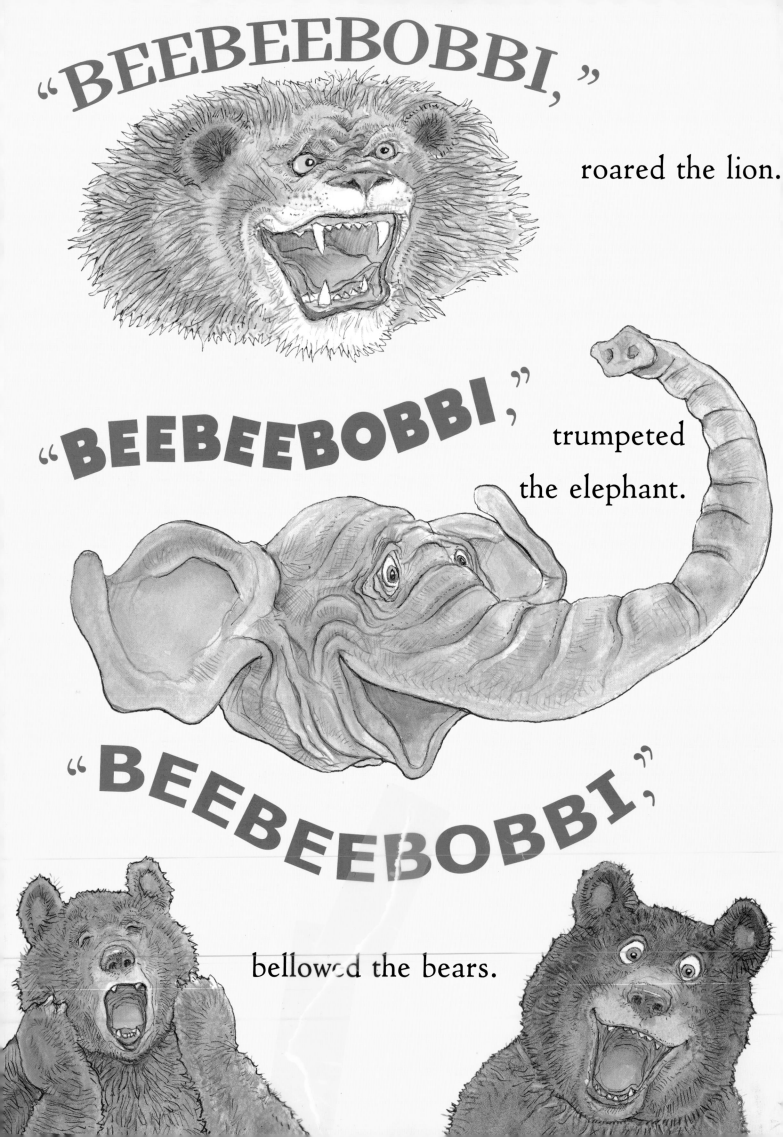

"BEEBEEBOBBI," roared the lion.

"BEEBEEBOBBI," trumpeted the elephant.

"BEEBEEBOBBI," bellowed the bears.

"BEEBEEBOBBIBOBBI! BEEBEEBOBBIBOBBI!"

sang all the animals together.

"QUIET!"

said the beebee bird.

"can't you see that I'm sleeping? It's time for my nap!"

"**BEE BEE BOBBI**," yelled the hippos.

"BEEBEE BOBBI," shrieked the seals.

"**BEE BEE BOBBI**," thundered the moose and the water buffalo.

"BEEBEEBOBBIBOBBI
BEEBEEBOBBIBOBBI,"
they roared.
The keeper came running
with his arms in the air.
"Something is wrong!"
he shouted.
"Something is very wrong
with the animals!
Whatever shall I do?"
And he jumped up
and down with alarm.
"BEEBEEBOBBI!!!"
sang the animals
all
day
long. . . .
And the baby beebee bird
simply couldn't sleep at all.

BEEBEEBOBBI
BEEBEEBOBBI
BEEBEEBOBBI
BEEBEEBOBBI
BEEBEEBOBBI
BEEBEEBOBBI
BEEBEEBOBBI
BEEBEEBOBBI
BEEBEEBOBBI
BEEBEEBOBBI
BEEBEEBOBBI

BEEBEEBOBBI
BEEBEEBOBBI
BEEBEEBOBBI
BEEBEEBOBBI
BEEBEEBOBBI
BEEBEEBOBBI
BEEBEEBOBBI
BEEBEEBOBBI
BEEBEEBOBBI
BEEBEEBOBBI
BEEBEEBOBBI

The sun went down and the moon came up.

BEEBEEBOBBI
BEEBEEBOBBI
BEEBEEBOBBI
BEEBEEBOBBI
BEEBEEBOBBI
BEEBEEBOBBI
BEEBEEBOBBI
BEEBEEBOBBI
BEEBEEBOBBI
BEEBEEBOBBI
BEEBEEBOBBI

BEEBEEBOBBI
BEEBEEBOBBI
BEEBEEBOBBI
BEEBEEBOBBI
BEEBEEBOBBI
BEEBEEBOBBI
BEEBEEBOBBI
BEEBEEBOBBI
BEEBEEBOBBI
BEEBEEBOBBI
BEEBEEBOBBI

"BEEBEEBOBBI,"
whispered the lion,
who was too tired to roar.

"BOBBIBEEBEE,"
sighed the bear
as he closed his eyes.

"BEE...BEE...BOB...BI...,"
mumbled the elephant,
half to himself.

And then . . . . all was still.

The moon shone down upon a sleeping zoo.

Not an ear or a tail or a whisker moved.

And high, high up in the linden tree a tiny bird,
inside a leaf, was fast asleep.

And now every day at the zoo you can hear
"beebeebobbibobbi beebeebobbibobbi"
in between the lion's roars.

But at night there is never a sound.

Nighttime is really best for sleeping . . .

especially for very little birds.